ARTHUR
AND THE
TRUE FRANCINE

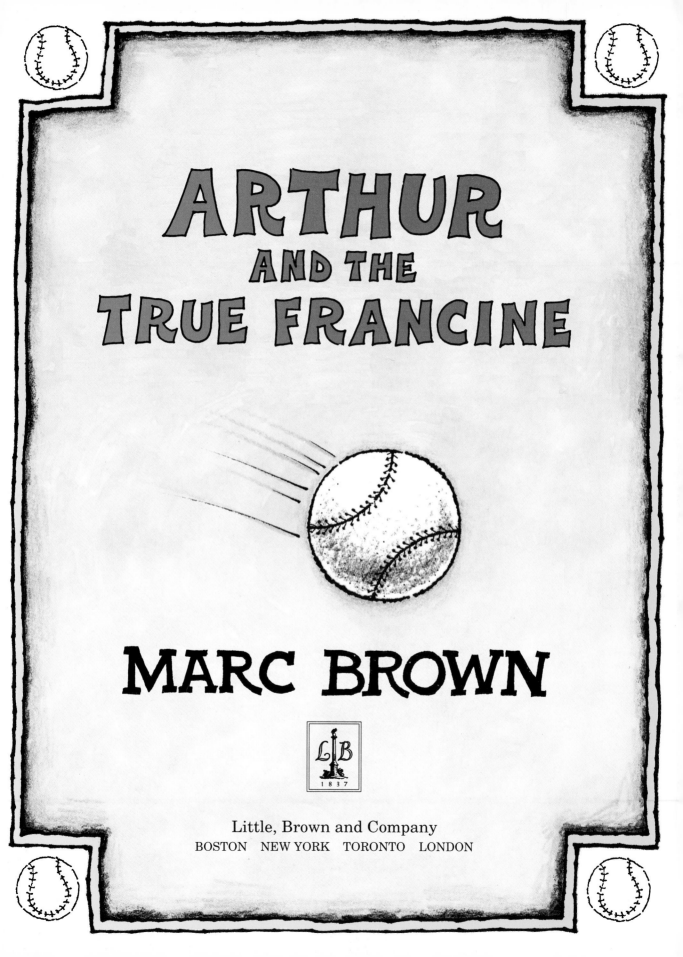

MARC BROWN

Little, Brown and Company
BOSTON   NEW YORK   TORONTO   LONDON

Library of Congress Cataloging-in-Publication Data
Brown, Marc Tolon.
Arthur and the true Francine

Summary: Francine and Muffy are good friends until Muffy lets
Francine take the blame for cheating on a test.
 ISBN 0-316-10949-5
  [1. Friendship–Fiction. 2. Honesty–Fiction. 3. Schools–Fiction.
4. Animals–Fiction] I. Title. II. Series.
[PZ7.B81618Tr 1987]   [E]   87-4136
ISBN 0-316-11136-8 (hc)
ISBN 0-316-10949-5 (pb)

10   9   8   7   6   5   4

WOR

*Published simultaneously in Canada
by Little Brown & Company (Canada) Limited*

Printed in the U.S.A.

For Terry Johnson,
Tara Sullivan,

and the real Mr. Ratburn
wherever he lurks.

It was the first day of school.
Everyone was worried about which
teacher they would get.
"I hope I get Miss Sweetwater," said Francine.

"Anyone's better than Mr. Ratburn," said
Arthur.
"He sleeps in a coffin," said Buster,
"and drinks human blood."

A big black car drove up.
"Who died?" said Francine.
"Maybe Mr. Ratburn!" said Arthur.
A girl got out.

"I'm Muffy Crosswire.
Where's the third grade, Antenna Ears?"
"Just ask for Mr. Ratburn!" said Buster.
They all laughed.

Everyone read Mr. Ratburn's class list first.
Francine groaned.
"Not Ratburn!" shouted Arthur.
"Impossible!" said Sue Ellen.

In Mr. Ratburn's class everyone sat in
alphabetical order.
No talking unless you raised your hand.
Muffy was teacher's pet.
Mr. Ratburn even believed her when she
said the cat ate her homework.

Francine always seemed to be in trouble.

But Francine and Muffy were best friends.
They both liked scary movies and
pistachio ice cream.
They even had the same middle name.
Alice.
Muffy called Francine "Slugger." She was
the best hitter on the softball team.
Francine called Muffy "Tinsel Teeth."

Muffy went to Francine's to study
for the big math test.
Francine studied very hard.
Muffy played with Francine's gerbil
and called strangers on the phone.

In the test Muffy copied
all Francine's answers. (Even the wrong
ones.)
Mr. Ratburn called Muffy and Francine to
his desk.
Muffy smiled. "I don't cheat," she said.
What could Francine say?

"Francine," he said, "I'll see *you* after
school every day this week."

Common American Turtles
1. Spotted Turtle
2. Common Mud Turtle
3. Spiny Soft-shelled Turtle
4. Western Painted Turtle
5. Three-toed Box
6. Red-eared
Report on
above
ALOHA

The big softball game against Miss Sweetwater's class was in three days.
"Francine, how could you do this to us?"
said Buster.
"Without you, we'll lose for sure."

Every day after school
Francine cleaned the boards and
watched the team practice.
Boy, did they need help.

Every day Muffy waited for Francine,
but Francine walked right past.
Muffy couldn't eat or sleep.
Should she tell Mr. Ratburn the truth?

It was the day of the big game.
Miss Sweetwater's class already had two
runs when Muffy ran to find Francine.
"Help, we need you," said Muffy.
"Mr. Ratburn says you're up!"

"Not unless you tell him the truth," said
Francine.
"Well, put on your mitt," said Muffy,
"I already did."

Francine saved the game with a home run.
Everyone cheered and shouted,
"We're number one!
We're number one!"
Muffy yelled, "Yea Francine! Way to go,
Slugger!"

Mr. Ratburn treated everyone to sodas
at Billy's Burger Barn.
"This is the best chocolate soda I've ever
tasted," said Muffy.

"Hey, Muffy, how'd you like to play for the team?" asked Buster.
"Yeah, we have just the spot for you," said Francine.

"Not so fast," said Mr. Ratburn. "Muffy will be washing the boards next week." Muffy whispered to Francine, "What will I play?"

"Scorekeeper," said Francine. "But you better learn to add. And no cheating!"